Today I Found a Unicorn

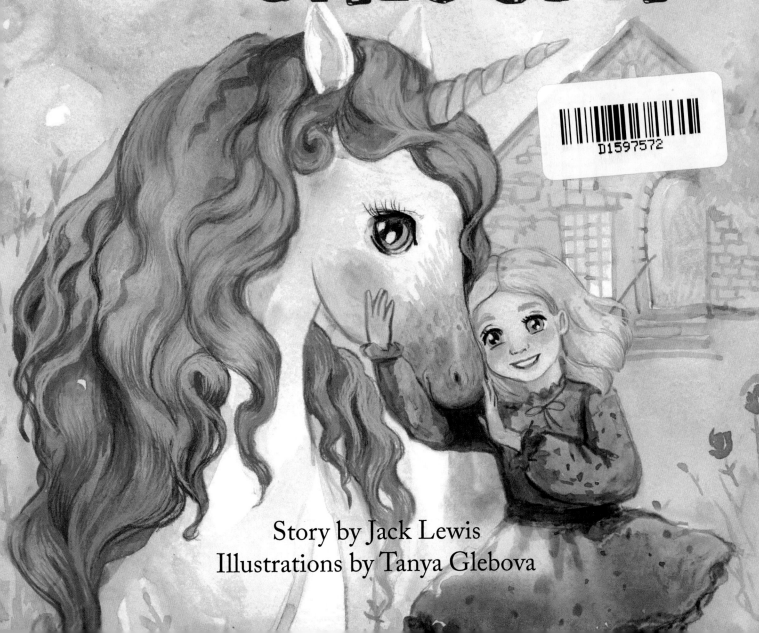

Story by Jack Lewis
Illustrations by Tanya Glebova

Dedication
For Maddie,
Never stop loving those Unicorns

For information contact:
Starry Dreamer Publishing, LLC 1603 Capitol Ave. Suite 310 A377
Cheyenne, Wyoming 82001
starrydreamerpub@gmail.com

Written by Jack Lewis
Illustrations by Tanya Glebova

ISBN: 978-1-952328-34-3 (Paperback) 978-1-952328-35-0 (Hardback)
Library of Congress Cataloging-in-Publication Data is available
10 9 8 7 6 5 4 3 2 1
First Edition: April 2020

STARRY DREAMER PUBLISHING

Today I found a Unicorn; she
was standing on our lawn.

Her golden horn was shiny, and it sparkled in the sunlight.

Can you believe it?
A Unicorn in my yard!

I ran inside and told my mom, "There's a Unicorn outside!"

But she didn't seem at all surprised. "That's lovely, dear," she said.

I went back outside and asked the Unicorn, "What's your name?"

But she just smiled at me and shook her silky mane.

I stroked her sides and asked her, "Would you like to stay and play?"

"It's a sunny summer day and we could picnic in the park."

She nodded her head excitedly and pawed the ground with her hoof. She was ready for an adventure and ready for some lunch.

So, I packed us sandwiches and apples, and a blanket big enough for two.

Then at the park, we ate our lunch. (Did you know Unicorns eat the same things we do?)

After lunch, we played a game. We played hide-and-seek. I really shouldn't brag, but I won every round.

Then we made silly faces and laughed until tears rolled down our cheeks. What happened next was magical; the Unicorn offered me a ride.

This fact may surprise you, but did you know Unicorns can fly?

Through the clouds we soared and swirled, flying circles in the sky.

The sun began to set, and twinkling stars popped out one by one. Evening had come, and it was time for me to go home.

We glided to my house and gently landed in the yard.

"Good night sweet Unicorn, and thanks for all the fun! Now the day is done, and I must go to bed."

Today I found a Unicorn; I wonder what I'll find tomorrow…

THE END

Enjoy these other great books by JACK LEWIS:

Never Bring a Zebracorn to School

Joy to the World: The Best Christmas Gift Ever

Wonderful World of Animals Series

Take a trip around the world to find the wildest, weirdest, and most adorable animals on the planet!

The Cutest Animals of the World

The Weirdest Animals of the World

The Most Dangerous Animals in the World

Today I Found... Series

Magical children's stories of friendship and the power of imagination!

Today I Found a Unicorn

Today I Found a Mermaid

Today I Found an Elf

Fun with Family Series

A wonderful way to celebrate each special person in our families!

I Love My Mommy

Made in the USA
Monee, IL
14 July 2022

99756031R00019